polly pocket ™

Whirlwind
World Tour

Adapted by Justine Fontes
Illustrated by MADA Design, Inc.

Manufactured and printed in China.
ISBN: 978-0-696-23646-4

We welcome your comments and suggestions.
Write to us at: Meredith Books, Children's Books,
1716 Locust St., Des Moines, IA 50309-3023.
Visit us online at: meredithbooks.com

Meredith® Books
Des Moines, Iowa

Hidden objects by page number: 3. on table; 4. in Lila's hands; 6. on Lila's wrist; 7. in Lila's hand; 9. in Samuel's hands; 10. on table; 12. in Lila's hands; 14. on Shani's wrist; 16. in Lea's hand; 18. in Shani's hands; 21. in Chrissy's hand; 22. in Chrissy's hands; 23. in Chrissy's hand; 24. on table; 25. on Polly's wrist; 26. in Chrissy's hands; 28. in Lea's hand; 29. by Chrissy's hand; 30. by Lea

Samuel, Polly Pocket's butler, has the perfect summer plan: a world tour with her peeps.

"Fantabulous!" Polly exclaims. "Where should we go first?"

Samuel replies, "Follow your whims to find serendipity."
"What's that?" asks Shani.
Samuel smiles. "Serendipity is travel's greatest treasure.
You'll know it when you see it."

Polly spins the globe. "I've always wanted to see Paris."
"We can leave right now," Samuel says.
"What about packing?" Crissy asks.
Polly says, "The Jumbo Jet has an onboard boutique and runway!"

Lila worries. "What if our look is totally yesterday?"
Polly laughs. "Then we'll just have to shop in Paris!"
Samuel smiles. "You're a natural at serendipity, Miss."

Everything about Paris is so quaint and chic. Polly wants to wrap up the whole city! But she settles for a few gorgeous outfits.

The girls want to see Paris Parisian style. So they ride bicycles along the famous river Seine.
Lila sighs. "I still can't believe I'm looking at the real Eiffel Tower!"

7

Next, the girls want to go to the Louvre Museum, so Lea asks a young woman for directions.

The woman exclaims, "Louis Vre? Oh, thank goodness you're here! I'm Collette. Let's get you ready. The show starts in . . . now!"

Collette thinks Polly and the Pockets are American models whose flight has been delayed. There is no time to explain the truth. So the girls strut down a real Parisian runway!

"A mistake that works out better than anything you could have planned. Is that serendipity?" Polly asks.

"That and more," Samuel replies.

"Where shall we go next?" Lea wonders.

Samuel shrugs. "Why not let chance decide? Write the names of a few places on pieces of paper. Toss the names in a hat. Then pick one!"

Polly picks a piece of paper. It reads, "Barcelona."

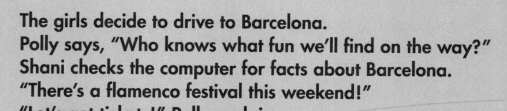

The girls decide to drive to Barcelona.
Polly says, "Who knows what fun we'll find on the way?"
Shani checks the computer for facts about Barcelona.
"There's a flamenco festival this weekend!"
"Let's get tickets!" Polly exclaims.

But the festival is sold out.
"Que será será," says Samuel. "Whatever will be will be."
Just then Lea cries, "Look!"

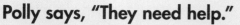

Polly says, "They need help."

Samuel agrees. The stranded travelers are members of Señorita Carlotta's Flamenco Dance Company. They are on their way to the festival.

"We'd be glad to take you there," Samuel says.

Señorita Carlotta is very grateful. "Muchas gracias!"

Then she turns to her dancers and smiles.

"Rápido!" Carlotta looks at Polly and adds, "Quickly!"

Everyone laughs.

Polly and her peeps see the flamenco festival with backstage passes!

Señorita Carlotta also invites them to the cast party. "And since you like to be . . . how do you say, stylish? Why don't you wear some of our costumes?"

Polly asks Samuel, "Is this serendipity?"

The dancing butler takes the rose out of his mouth to reply. "At its finest, Miss."

In Rome, Polly and her peeps visit the city's most famous landmark, the Colosseum. Lea says, "It's cool to imagine real, live gladiators fighting in there."

Shani rubs her stomach. "I wonder what ancient Romans ate."

Just then Polly sees a man dressed like a gladiator. He is handing out flyers for Toga Tony's Ancient Roman Restaurant.

19

The girls soon find out that ancient Romans didn't sit on chairs to eat. Instead, they reclined on couches. Lila whispers, "What if ancient Roman food is totally gross?"

"Then we'll order room service from the hotel," Polly replies.

But the food was great!

Polly sighs. "I almost feel like I really am in ancient Rome."

Samuel smiles. "Travel broadens the mind."

Modern Romans love to
drive very fast. Polly and her
peeps drive as fast as they dare.
Then Polly says, "Let's take our wheels
out in the countryside."
    Soon they were far north of busy Rome.

The girls don't care where they are going. Shani sees a sign written in several languages. They are in Switzerland!

In a tiny mountain town, a flock of sheep blocks their way.

Samuel suggests, "Shall we try that cafe?"
Hilda Rottenmeier, their waitress, is excited to meet American girls. "My shift is over soon. Would you like to meet my parents and see our farm?"

Hilda's parents invite Polly and her peeps to stay for dinner.

"But first we must bring in the sheep," says Mr. Rottenmeier. "Would you like to help?"

Hilda and her father already have some amazing four-legged help. Polly and her friends watch the sheepdog herd the flock into the barn. They also have a great time playing with the sheepdog's puppies. Polly says, "Making new friends is so much cooler than just being a tourist."

Mr. Rottenmeier lets the girls pet some lambs. He says, "Each spring we shear the sheep. By fall, a nice thick coat grows back."

Hilda's mother shows the girls how to spin and knit wool. "I think it's nice to keep up the old ways," she says.

Polly giggles. "I feel like a fairy-tale princess."

The next day they are back in the U.S.A.
"I can't believe we were in Switzerland this morning,"
Crissy says.
"And petting lambs yesterday," Lea adds.

"I'll never look at a sweater the same way again," says Polly. Then she winks at Samuel. "I'll never look at anything the same old way again. From now on I'll be searching for serendipity wherever I go!"

Start your fabulicious™
Polly Pocket™
collection with these Spectabulous titles!

Pollyworld™
8x8

Polly's Fabulous
Pet Palace
8x8

The Tricky Tryouts
Early Reader

Pollyworld™
Early Reader

Polly and the
Makeover Mess
Early Reader

CLD0132_0607